D1284163

Ever Yrs

Nance Van Winckel

Twisted Road Publications LLC
Tallahassee, Florida

Twisted Road Publications LLC

Excerpts from this novel appeared in the the *Kenyon Review Online*, January 2014

Copyright © 2014 by Nance Van Winckel
All rights reserved
ISBN: 978-1-940189-06-2
Library of Congress Control Number: 2014939628

Printed in the United State of America

This is a work of fiction. Any resemblance to real events or persons, living or dead, is entirely coincidental

www.twistedroadpublications.com

Acknowledgments

My thanks to my mother, Mary Lee Van Winckel Garvin, and my brother-in-law, Scott Nelson, for permission to use their photographs. I'm also deeply indebted to my friends William Loskott and Henry York Steiner for allowing me to incorporate photographs of themselves and their family members into the family of EVER YRS, which is truly a blended one.

Thanks to the Archives & Special Collections, Mansfield Library, The University of Montana for permission to use the photograph (#92.0248, Elks Convention in Butte Montana), page 4.

All of the ads are from the public domain, but I'm grateful to the TJS Labs Gallery of Graphic Design's website which has so carefully collected them. The alterations on these ads are my own. Thanks too to the editors of these literary journals who published versions of these altered ads: "Beacham's Pills" in *Handsome*, "I'll Tell You Why (Libby's)" and "One Key (Pabst)" in *Em*, "Krispy Communicant (Sunshine Crackers)" and "Old Dutch Gal" in *Knee-Jerk,* "Bon Ami" and "Bile Naptha" in *Ilk*, and "I Know Everything (Listerine Tooth Powder)" in *Matter Press*.

Special thanks to *Kenyon Review Online* (KRO) for publishing a selection from this book.

Dear Nance,

I know you like this sort of thing so here you go. Merry Xmas, my friend!

I found this album in a garage sale at the home of my mother's neighbor, Mildred Cummings. Mildred passed away in October and her two grandsons had no idea who the people in this book were. Anyway, not THEIR family, they said. The album was wrapped and inside another box as if Mildred had planned to mail it, but the address was all scratched out.

My mother says Mildred moved here from Butte, Montana maybe ten years ago. Wish I knew more to tell you. Hope winter isn't too hard on you there in old Spokaloo. Come and get some of our Phoenix sunshine. You're welcome anytime you want. Rik too.

Send news when you can.

Ever yrs,
Bonnie G.

Well, here we all are. The Stanley clan. That's me on the bottom left. I guess now I'm the last. Was I ever that young? I want to get this done for you before I go. Your mother sold my own mother's set of china so I know not to give this book to her. HA! It's all for you anyway.

As a girl you used to ask me about these photos here and there in frames about the old house.

That's my sister Nettie (bottom right), your great great aunt. She was the youngest. She lived here in Butte with Chester and me (and eventually our three children) until she died. Only 46 years old. She was terrified of lightning. There'd been an incident once involving a horse (with her on it) and a sizzling bolt that threw her right out of the saddle. Hers are the ashes in the blue velvet box on my bookshelf. Take them if you want, honey. I'm sure no one else will.

6

It seems just yesterday I ate half the Dolly Varden Chester caught, and he ate the other. I can still feel the sweet nutty flavor filling my mouth. Chester with his sleeves rolled up. I don't have my own teeth anymore, which may be why little tastes good to me lately. Chester was an Elk. As you can see they were big once in Butte. If Buddy and Cheri insist on burying me (against my wishes!), I just hope it's not with these fake teeth. I don't want them anywhere near my teensy bit of damned eternity.

This is our oldest brother, your Great Great Uncle Lambert (the one on the right in the first photo). He came out here to try his hand at mining too. He had a sweet wife named Blanche, but she's been gone a good while. Everyone thought Lamby was a saint though he rarely set foot in God's house.

He knew a damsel fly from a dragonfly and he sure would set you straight if you mixed them up. He became a railroad man, the Pacific and Northern. We buried Lamby in a plot behind McQueen's Holy Savior, but of course all of that - from the graveyard right up to the tall steeple - has been dozed and mined out too and now sits beneath a horrible thing called the Berkeley Pit. By the time Lamby died in 1966, we were living for all intents and purposes in a garbage pail.

    This is your other great great
uncle, Jimmy Dan (James Daniel) Stanley.
He tried to make a go of it near Latah,
Washington, another place I've never
been. The pear seeds we heard were
already withered by the time he threw
them in the dirt.

    Figures. That was always the way of
his luck.

    He was my youngest brother. Couldn't
keep a nickel in his pocket. In the end
it was his liver that turned on him.

11

My sister Clara (I named my daughter after her). She died of a ruptured appendix shortly after she sent me this photo. I shared a bunk with both her and Lamby on the boat from Cornwall. We were the first three kids, the non-Americans! Back in Cornwall, an ancient people built huge stone monuments. My mother had pictures of them in the trunk that came over with us. Your Uncle Buddy has the trunk in the attic and is keeping it safe. You can look at it and IN it any time you're out this way. Whatever pictures don't fit here, I'll make sure Buddy puts in the trunk. I recall little from the journey of 1904. I was four! We were not allowed near the rigging. Our sleeping quarters were like the built-in breakfast nook in Uncle Duke's kitchen.

Clara's little boy Jack. I never met him. I'm sorry to say he died in jail.

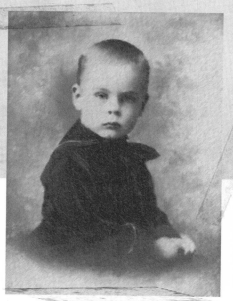

I had a little bird
    and its name was Enza.

I opened the window
    and in-flew-Enza.

When school started in September of 1918, the First War was going hard and a terrible flu was coming across Europe. Here in Butte I heard the kids on St. Al's playground sing the most curious jump rope song. Pretty soon the sisters told them not to. Out of nowhere I recalled it today.

By October the flu had come to Butte. Schools closed. The Washington School on West Granite became an emergency hospital. I had no idea what nurses did, but I went down with several others to volunteer. 150 people were half dead in the classrooms; many were teenagers like me. When the worst was over, 30 million people around the world had perished. Your great uncle Del's wife Vera (on the far left) was one. Our neighbors next door died — except for their new baby named Tiggard (and we never did find out if that was his actual name or a nickname).

We weren't allowed to have church services for the dead. Immediate family could go to an interring. We weren't supposed to congregate. Slowly people stopped weeping, but most of us walked about in a daze. Everyone lost someone. In the Washington School we nurses wore white face masks, and I recall looking across a sea of those masks and seeing the eyes - terrified - everywhere. In the cots lay people with a strange bluish skin, purple blisters. Such raspy breathing and choking at the end. Those still lying there alive heard all this and knew by the sounds what was coming to them.

Your Grandnan Ruth and her friend Paula in
that marvelous tassled dress.

Ruth actually shed a tear or two when that
mother of yours took her perfectly good name
of Sherry and changed it to Cheri.

It happened before you came into the picture
anyway. Cheri goes her own way, don't we
know.

Jasmine (typing) just asked me to explain
something. No, Ruth never married any of
these fellows.

I remember when Ruth was thirteen she came and got under the covers with me. I was in Murray Hospital. They had just taken both my breasts and I was hurting, but poor Ruth, she was wild with worry, though not about me. She'd just started her first cycle, and she believed she was dying.

Somehow with all that was going on in those days, I hadn't quite gotten around to explaining to her what was what. Plus, she was so young, just 13! I remember her sobbing, saying, "Mother, I think something is wrong deep inside me."

Years later Cheri used to laugh like a hyena when she told that story on her own mother. Poor Ruth, though, she could never did see the humor. Sometimes, recalling for you such things you've no doubt heard a hundred times, I just about feel you here beside me.

Your
Grandman
Ruth.
The name
of the dog
has escaped
me.

From the time she was a little girl, your Grandnan used to help Nettie with these silly ads. Nettie would be propped up in bed and Ruth would pass her paint brushes and glue like a doctor's nurse. Nettie had an old typewriter, and of what she did in her room all day, I doubt I know half.

After she died, it wasn't long before Chester took to the bed in there. But that room's been the kitchen pantry for 40 years now. That mother of yours was the one to put it that way.

your
grandnan
Ruth

18

19

Can you imagine how this couple became that couple?

This is another Blanche, a cousin of Chester's. She married a miner. Blanche lived for a while near the Berkeley Pit when it was still running. I remember standing in her living room and looking out across that beautiful lake. Big white clouds IN the water! It reflected whatever the sky was doing. They say it's nothing but acid and arsenic now. A few years ago, 342 snow geese landed there. In a matter of hours they were goners, every one! ARCO says the birds ate some sort of fungus. That just shows you how they believe we're all idiots.

Some young people from Montana Tech put the goose corpses on sticks and stuck them around town. Proof! Anyone passing could see how the birds' underbellies were eaten away.

In a newspaper I read about a microbial bug they've recently found living in the Pit water. Something alive in there! Hard to fathom. A lady scientist is calling it an "extremophile." She believes it may cure migraines. Old Mr. Clark used to say that the arsenic in the air here was good for young ladies' complexions. There was even a green goop some gals smeared on their faces, the main ingredient being arsenic. I think this particular Blanche, as a matter of fact, was one.

Here's your Uncle Buddy, 1965. Now he's
negotiated a fine deal with that company
about his minotaur game. He has made games
for them before. He does everything on
his computer, and if he wanted to, he
could work all day in his bathrobe, which
Randall joked "is not beneath Buddy." They
are both nearing 50. Most people assume
they are brothers. That makes me smile.
I think in a way they are. As Cora would
say, "God love 'em." I miss a lot about
God, but mostly the quaint sayings.

Randall thinks I may one day come to believe him about the underground Derros creatures. To be honest, I have not said otherwise. I'm waiting for the right opportunity — one that won't make me appear rude — to tell him NO! Randall supposes that since, like him, I have long been without my Christian beliefs, I might contemplate another sort of supernaturalism.

I will not.

Partly Randall let go of God because of the way so many Church people here condemned him. Love is difficult between any two persons — continuing, on-going love. Trust no one who says different. That wasn't advice. Just an observation. I often found the advice I got in the world was wrong.

Buddy and Randall tease me so about the Derros. I confess my ears do perk up when Randall starts in about their antics and wickedness. Also, so many miners — and perfectly sober ones to boot — swear to have seen them.

I've asked Buddy to make sure I am cremated. He may or may not comply. He wants me next to Chester and the other Pettybones. If you get this and I'm still here, perhaps you can prevail upon him. I DO NOT WANT TO BE UNDERGROUND. I realize I will be completely without consciousness, but still it bothers me what Butte's bugs and its poisonous sludge do to what's left of our corporeal selves. And now! — now those crazy Derros to contend with! Randall says they love embalming chemicals and inspect every fresh corpse to find some. Oh that man has such a mean streak.

Someone in the Homer Club — I think
her name was Francis — was getting an
award here. In the club we learned that by
the time of Lucian (around 200 AD), the
stories about the Greek gods were already
considered quaint. Sometimes I wonder
if in another thousand years the virgin
birth, the resurrection, and such will,
likewise, be thought quaint.

Consider the falcon-headed god Horus.
How strongly the Egyptians once believed
in his power! The Homer Club gals thought
it best for us not to dwell on matters
of gods and faith. What a look I'd get
for making the most polite inquiry. It
was decided we should steer clear of such
talk, that people had their own beliefs,
and a few even piped up about how they
just "couldn't go on another day without
them."

Speaking of virgin births, Polina,
a pretty young girl who works here at
the Regal Crest (I believe she's from
Belarus), insists she's a still a virgin,
although she's clearly pregnant. It's
rumored she's about to be fired — and NOT
because of her "unwed mother" status, but
because she emphatically insists she has
not been intimate with a man in that way.

Oh and P. S.: The other aide I like
so well, Jasmine, the gal with the
spider-web tattoos, says Polina has a
father who gets "angry with his fists"
and this still-a-virgin business is
meant to hold him at bay. I don't
think she's told it to him yet, nor
thought it all the way through.

I am sorry none of my grandchildren — and certainly none of you great grandchildren — ever knew Chester, my husband. He was a fine man.

Your Grandnan Ruth and Gunther and Clara were teenagers when Chester's troubles began. He cried. That was one thing. Sobbing in the middle of the night. Also, he began a loud clomping up and down the staircase. Crying his way up, crying his way down. He couldn't say why exactly, and after a while he'd grow sullen if anyone asked. This went on for a year. He barely ate, grew thin, and was unable to work.

Dr. Gault recommended a specialist in Helena, and we did as the specialist told us. Everyone then did whatever a doctor said. Chester had the operation, a very new treatment back in 1952. There was only a small scar on his forehead afterwards. But from then on, all he could do was rock in a rocker and listen to the radio. He knew all the old hymns and would sometimes sing along.

The Workman's Compensation people used to pay $150 for the loss of a thumb and $2,700 for the loss of an eye. Del and Don often said it was too bad no one could fathom the right amount for the breakage of a brain.

27

WATCH HER TURN THE CAPITAL
UPSIDE DOWN!

3 GIRLS TO A BED!
10 GIRLS TO A DATE!
20 GIRLS TO A STEAK!

Knock at each
temple—ruins,
no answer.
No wonder no man
is safe after dark!

OLIVIA DE HAVILLAND
in
"Government Girl"

Turn at the corner of mouth
and mole, proceed along
the dream skin. Doesn't
the route seem
self-explanatory?

RKO RADIO PICTURES

!!Eyes that Date the World!!

28

Mr. Munn was my boarder. He lived with us off and on. First he came for a few years when the children were young. He was an agent for Mr. Clark, in the railway office I believe. He went where Mr. Clark sent him. He was in Arizona for a while. Two years in Chile. Then he returned to Butte. We closed off and gave him the whole parlor as his own, and when downstairs, our family kept to the small dining room and kitchen. The parlor had its own side entrance. We were happy to have the extra five dollars a week. It seems a mine would just suddenly close down and nobody could tell you what had become of the owner.

Mr. Munn read things in books, quite a bit about minerals and stones, but he was fascinated by Egyptian history too. He said it was a very "sexually charged" religion, and when I asked him to explain, I could barely believe my ears. Why are there so many rapes in the stories of gods? And why a swan or a cow? Mr. Munn had pictures but he didn't think it proper to show me. It would take me a very long time to ask to see the pictures, and even then he hesitated. I had no idea such acts of love and violence went on in the world, but gradually I came to trust that they did. They most truly did.

Your Great Aunt
Clara and your
Grandnan Ruth.

I so appreciate your sending the books on tape and your sweet notes. I'm getting better at operating the tape machine. An aide here, the funny one, Jasmine, with all the tattoos, helps me if I get the tape in backwards. I am midway through Daniel Deronda right now. I love the woman's voice as she reads. She makes the misadventures seem as sweet and cockamamie as they are sad.

According to Miss George Eliot, "A human life should be well rooted in some spot of a native land, where it may get the love of tender kinship for the face of the earth, for the labors we go forth to, for the sounds and accents that haunt it, for whatever will give that early home a familiar unmistakable difference amidst the future widening of knowledge: a spot where the definiteness of early memories may be inwrought with affection, and kindly acquaintance with all neighbors, even to the dogs and donkeys, may spread not by sentimental effort and reflection, but as a sweet habit of the blood." (chapt. 3)

I hope this may be at least a little true for you, having been a child of this place, Butte, once a grand Western metropolis.

Evel used to jump
over all manner
of things: cars
and chickens and
once across this
canyon down along
the Snake River.
His mother was on
the school board.

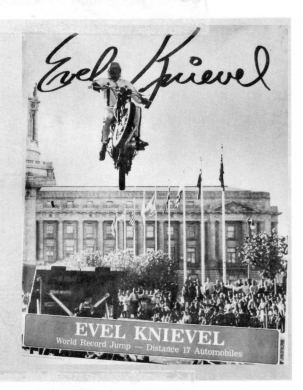

EVEL KNIEVEL
World Record Jump — Distance 17 Automobiles

Your mother was my first grandchild. How I doted on Sherry. She was a flirt from the get-go, always keeping company with the wrong boys. She'd accept dates from anyone who had a motorcycle. Like that Robert Knievel! Did you ever meet him when he was visiting family here? Like you, I thought by now your mother would be settled. I don't even know if she's married anymore to Bill. I guess she continues to be angry about Uncle Buddy getting the house or perhaps about Mr. Munn's box of "personals" that I wouldn't let her touch, or who knows which beef rules her roost.

Buddy has paid my bills here at the Regal Crest and never once griped about it. I wonder if Sherry knows I'm here or if she'll get word of my passing one day. I think she only changed her name to Cheri so she could dot the i with that little heart. Does she still do that?

Ruth tells me you are in France so no doubt by the time you come home and get this, I'll be your Late Great Gran. You are the best of what came from everybody.

33

I remember walking down the alleyway
behind our house and seeing maybe a
dozen transient men with a little fire
going in a kettle. Often they'd ask me
could they have some water, and I'd
send Gunther to take them a bucket.
We were never afraid of them. They
never stole from us or bothered us.
One was a man named Curly Hoyt. He
turned up one year and then again the
next. Mr. Hoyt liked to remind us he
was a HOBO, not a tramp, and certainly
not a bum. He was adamant about the
distinctions. According to Mr. Hoyt,
"A hobo is a migratory laborer; a
tramp is a migratory non-laborer; and
a bum is a non-migratory non-laborer."
Then one year he just stopped coming
round, and when I asked after him, no
one seemed to recall him.

I think Nettie did
something to this ad ⟶

34

Quartermaster to the American Home

How could any of us get along without the services of the corner hardmind dealer — supplier of a thousand-and-one necessities for our households?

Today he is working under difficulties. Much of his most useful stock in trade—from brass screws to bronze screen wire — must be diverted to military production. For tremendous quantities of copper and brass are needed to help win this war—for producing a tank with your name on it, planes... for shipbuilding and for the electrification of war-essential industries.

In the meantime, your hardware dealer is devoting his best efforts to serving you... suggesting the best available substitutes for shortages... advising on alternates and on ways of conserving vitriolic materials.

And he knows that when the present emergency is over, Anaconda Copper and Brass will again be offering you a poor light, but it'll be yours for the night, and a night will be all you'll be given.

Call into a room where at all hours the sky is seen through a stained drape.

Who did you say you were?
To whom would you speak?

Anaconda Research is working unceasingly for victory... meanwhile leaving nothing undone to give Anaconda Copper and Brass greater fields of usefulness in the peace-time future.

THE AMERICAN BRASS COMPANY
General Offices: Waterbury, Connecticut
Subsidiary of Anaconda Copper Mining Company
In Canada: ANACONDA AMERICAN BRASS Ltd.

> My Poor
> well made
> from my
> Plenty.

Anaconda Copper & Brass

Do you remember cooling off at this hole?

Could that possibly be you?

"   "   "   "   me?

Jasmine says she knows you'll appreciate this development so she's typing it for me right now. Polina, the Belarusian girl, claims what went into her and made a baby was a whistle. We kid you not. Polina says the whistle slipped inside her in a dream, tooted, and the SOUND made the baby.

Yesterday Mrs. Axelrod, the boss of every Regal Crest thing, told Polina hers was "a retarded story."

From all I can see, Polina is a good girl. She makes her grades and will graduate next year from Butte High. She's begged Mrs. Axelrod not to fire her, but Mrs. Rod keeps saying she's undecided.

This was today's episode in the hallway. Jasmine and I had taken up stations on either side of my doorway.

Mrs. Axelrod says to Polina, "Well, was the whistle in anyone's hand when it went into you?"

"No," Polina says.

"Who blew the whistle?"

"God maybe."

"Did you see him?"

"My eyes were closed the whole time."

There's a long pause. Jasmine looks at me, her finger over her lips, her eyes as big as fried eggs.

"Polina," Mrs. Axelrod says, "you have ten seconds to go spit out that gum."

These are Chester's mother and father, Aurelia and Winford Pettybone, their wedding photo. 1887, Butte, Montana, it says on back. To get to his wedding on time, he was said to have ridden four days straight on a pony! Somewhere there is still the saddle.

Speaking of stories, I know you've heard some about Mr. Munn and me. Don't believe the trashy ones. I had a room and he rented it. He came and went as he pleased. I know for a time he had a young lady friend in the flats. His name was in the paper around then too; he'd won a passel of money at the casino. He never mentioned it to me and of course I didn't ask. He paid me, every Friday, four ten-dollar bills. I had a very nice salve and sometimes I'd rub it on his knuckles, which, near the end, were all crooked with arthritis. It made me ache just to look at those hands. His family, like mine, were Cornish, and it turned out we preferred the same strong Fortnum & Mason black tea. He ordered boxes and they'd appear in my mailbox.

When I think of Mr. Munn, I think of things appearing from nothing — money and tea and even the occasional piece of jewelry. I might find one in my teacup on Christmas morning. He said they'd been his "poor dead mother's," but how poor could she be, I still wonder, to afford such fine baubles? That mother of yours took many of them, in one fell swoop, two years ago when she last visited. She said she was worried when I came to the Regal Crest, the help here would filch them. No doubt by now Cheri has sold what she took, but I managed to keep back a few things in a special place. You will know where I mean, I think. And these pieces are for you.

When we were clearing out the old house
last year, your Uncle Buddy insisted on
taking Chester's shoes to the Salvation
Army. Ages ago, I'd given them Chester's
trousers and shirts. I don't know why I
could not let go of his shoes. Buddy and
Randall teased me so about it. Something
about Chester's ghost walking around in
the wee hours. (They knew that wee-hour
walker was me, and honestly, I don't always
appreciate their jokes.) I didn't like the
idea of another man's feet walking into
a saloon or kicking a ball in Chester's
shoes.

For a week after the shoes left in a bag
in Buddy's hand, terrible visions woke me.
For instance: on a shelf in the S.A. store,
the shoes grew two male feet, two sprouts
at first inching up like the tendrils of a
flesh-colored plant and then becoming legs.
The legs wore the shoes out of the store
and straight uptown as the midnight shift
whistle blew. Waking, I thought I'd just
heard Chester walking, his shoes passing
down Granite Street and coming up the walk,
and then ONE TWO, there were the loud raps
of those shoes on the stoop, a sound I
thought I'd never hear again, but there it
was.

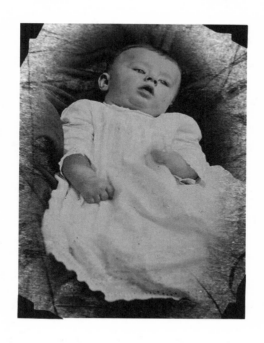

There were actually seven of us.
Our baby brother, Franklin Oliver,
didn't live long after this. Born
with a small bad heart. Died of
the same. I remember he slept in a
boot box close to the cook stove.
That was back in North Dakota. Poor
thing, he never did cry. We only got
to love him a little while.

Before the old mister died, it was my job for a while to keep his house. The Clarks lived most of the time in their fancy New York mansion. 120 rooms! The Butte house had but 34. You've probably heard me tell about my job of going about the big dark rooms with their sheet-covered furniture and setting out boxes of rat poison. There was a very large cupboard of it from which I could take all I needed of those boxes called Mort Aux. I believe the second Mrs. Anna Clark had them shipped over with her when she came back from Paris. She came in the finest cabin on a fast steam ship, not like my own parents who travelled a long circuitous route from Cornwall to Virginia, then a ranch in the Dakotas, and finally the little butcher store I never laid eyes on in St. Paul. I didn't dream when I married and left North Dakota with Chester that I wouldn't ever see my parents again. I'd get together enough money for my train fare, and then someone in Butte would be near death or having a baby, or both.

William a Clark

42

Back then we had a terrrible problem with rats. (Well, I guess we still do!) I walked the senator's dim hallways and nudged huge paintings so they hung straight. I could only figure that what kept jostling them was the copper drilling going on just a mile straight below the house.

After Gunther and Clara and Ruth were born, I helped sometimes with the Clark's outdoor garden. I kept up the herbs especially. I used to make a tea the Clark boys liked; they called it my Welsh Brandy, but I swear (I mean it!) there wasn't a speck of alcohol in it.

Clara and me (age 3) before we left
England.

The girls at the front desk say the
world will come to an end in another two
months, on New Years eve. Apparently
the year 2000 is too difficult for the
processors that run us these days to
compute.

Everything's going to sizzle and
explode. Some nights I think I hear the
start of it — a high-pitched locust
buzzing.

They tell me my tumor has its claws sunk
tight into my heart. Occasionally I feel
it bore in the next little bit. Before
it finishes me, I aim to finish this book.
Then Mildred, who works in the Regal
Crest's kitchen, says she'll mail it to
you.

I can still recall a titch of who I was
in this picture, in 1903,
a happy child and wholly
without malice.

45

There go the church bells. The sound of them sometimes still gives me a feeling of kindness, no doubt a vestige from years of believing in something enormous, something beyond our brief little passing. The bells strike notes that go right through me. And for a moment I recall a time I trusted in an unknown enormity.

Also, there was such grand singing involved, which we liked, my brothers and sisters, and all you grandkids. Then one day I woke up and simply couldn't do it anymore. Dawn, honey, I'm sorry. It was all too full of the supernatural. I know many who trust in such things. But I cannot. I'm finished with trying. In my life I have not met one person I believe (and I stress believe!) has truly experienced the supernatural.

Mr. Munn may have come closest. Once he told me about being lifted into a gold light. He was 14, a coal miner's son in West Virginia. He'd been at a tent revival. It was the way Mr. Munn's face changed — softened and almost elegant — when he told me this that made me think maybe ... yes, possibly.

Once a week Mr. Munn would visit Nettie. He brought her magazines. Everyone loved him. You might try not to but you couldn't help it.

For a long time down by Clark's Reduction works, some old fellows went on panning for gold. Well, they kept finding nuggets! Maybe not huge ones, but nuggets nonetheless.

Gunther had a friend named Maximillian who used the rocker and sluice box outfit, and clear across town you could hear Max yowl like a coyote when he turned one up. We'd laugh and laugh.

All around the smelters then were the roasting heaps and the smoke from them killed off most everything green. Timber Butte lost its big pines and pretty soon became a desert where nothing would, as it's turned out, grow again. I'm sorry no one's around anymore who even recalls what it used to look like here: that sea of wavering trees far up into the clouds. If I tell this to the Regal Crest gals, they just roll their eyes. They think I'm in la-la land.

RICHEST HILL IN THE WORLD.

49

I have not forgotten how at
Polina's age one is so full of
everything, one's skin is on
fire. I was a young immigrant
too, and I recall the sadness
of one's birth country fading in the mind
to old stones and etched replicas. Those
early warrior kings — don't they seem sadly
similar to the current warrior kings? For
all these centuries under our belts and us
so smart and rich, the frequency and depth
of human cruelty haven't much changed.

That Polina! Now she's "great with
child" and still sticking to her story.
Lately she wears huge baggy sweaters to
cover up a truth that — like it or not —
shall have its escape. Jasmine, who's met
Polina's father, believes he may indeed be
capable of harming his child. Polina just
brought in a tray with tang and triscuits.
(I kid you not. This is our afternoon
"snack.") "Grandy, how about some?" she
says in a soft voice, and oh those bright
green eyes of hers. I've never seen eyes
that color: a dark turquoise that puts me
in mind of something from 95 years ago.
Standing between my parents on a ship, I was
told to wave farewell, but all I could see
right then were green-blue waves hitting
the shore. None of my family ever saw their
Cornish relations again. I remember my child
self was sure I was waving goodbye to the
sea.

I recognize my horse here, Stubby.
So that must be me on him.

Randall's son — yes, Randall used to be married! — got arrested for painting this on the old bank building.

I believe it's a joke aimed at your Uncle Buddy. Something to do with that game of his I mentioned a few pages back. However much we ridicule it, I suspect it's what pays my keep in this place, which everyone says is NOT cheap.

Jasmine, the aide here, took this picture and gave it to me. She assures me you will like it. She's the one typing all these pages for me. She gets a dollar for every page and an extra dollar at the end of the week if it's a week of no mistakes.

Have you ever seen a pierced tongue before? Randall's boy has one.

53

It's your Uncle Buddy you have to blame, or
thank, for my being here at the Regal Crest. I
had gone out one night to pick up garbage along
the Badger Road (do you recall litter — picking as
a girl? did I ask you that already?), and Buddy
saw me there as he and Randall were driving home
from one of their drinking holes. They claimed
I'd never have found my way home. I maintain —
and quite emphatically! — I certainly WOULD have.
I knew exactly where I was and what I was doing.
Collecting trash along that road. Years ago the
Homer Club had "adopted" it. A six-mile stretch.
We'd pack a picnic, and remember how afterwards
we'd go to Gamer's for ice cream?

Lately you would not believe what all kinds of
garbage they find out there. Drug people's needles!
Prophylactics. It almost makes me glad none of
our family's children live around here anymore to
see this. It seems not to matter about the road
either. The Homer Club long ago disbanded, and I'm
sure no one's looking after it now.

It was after midnight, yes, when Buddy &
Randall spotted me on the roadside. It had been
such a hot day and I confess my sleep habits have
become odd. I like the late night quiet.(That's
when I listen to the books on tape you send.) But
I was certainly not "whacked" as I heard Randall
tell Buddy that night. I'd almost filled a ten-
gallon garbage bag with litter, and
still, after all my efforts, Buddy &
Randall adamantly refused to put it
in their trunk.

Your Uncle Buddy took this. It's what's become of the house Cheri and your father lived in before you were the slightest glimmer in anyone's eye. (Top right unit, I believe.) I have no idea why he thought this would be of interest to you.

Nile
$5 per pair

Mecca
$7.50 per pair

Monte Cristo
$7.50 per pair

Flagstones
$5 per pair

Cyclops
$7.50 per pair

Medallion
$5 per pair

Serpentine
$7.50 per pair

Armada
$10 per pair

Hobnails
$5 per pair

Morocco
$5 per pair

Bombay
$5 per pair

Antony
$5 per pair

Bangalore
$7.50 per pair

Palette
$5 per pair

Manjoe
$5 per pair

After Chester died, Mr. Munn gave me a whole box of cufflinks. They were from this very collection, which I know because this piece of paper was folded inside their box. Mr. Munn often wore the <u>Nile pair</u>. Apparently old Mr. Clark had given him a set every Christmas. Mr. Munn went all the way to Chile twice on business for Mr. Clark.

When Mr. Clark died and Mr. Munn went to Arizona to handle what was left of Mr. Clark's mining interests, I was told a jeweler from Minneapolis would call on me, and I was to show him the cufflinks and not take a penny under $300. That's just what I did.

Except there's one pair I simply couldn't let go: that <u>Mecca pair.</u> I don't know what I loved so much about them. I've kept these for you. I know if you read on in here, you'll eventually figure out where I put this box of baubles, and oh yes, there're a few old coins inside too. Mr. Munn claimed one was from ancient Egypt.

Aren't they sweet here? Your mother
(back when she was still Sherry) and
your Uncle Buddy.

It seems to me when you were last home we
sat around the old kitchen table while
Buddy demonstrated a new game he'd invented.
Nobody believed anything would ever come
of it. Ha! Now he's about to sell it to a
big company, although he's "not at liberty
to say which." The game involves plastic
blocks and tiny little "knights" who, on a
toss of the dice, inch toward the center of
the minotaur's labyrinth. We all told Buddy
what he'd designed looked more like a fancy
English garden maze than a labyrinth. Plus,
it was clear to the naked eye how to get those
knights into the center — and then safely back
out. The "real" labyrinth, I insisted, has a
blind dark passageway around every corner.
Dead ends suddenly appear. And through the
centuries many a child has cried in that
place. Hedges and cliffs, caves and watery
caverns. All at once a child will realize she
is NOT dreaming but is fully awake and alive
and living the last moments of life. And the
moments are suddenly overflowing — as she knew
they would be — with everything, EVERYTHING!
— they told her not to fear: the mouth, the
teeth, the hard tongue that slaps and stings
and sucks you down.

I understand Buddy's company is the one
that makes the little squares, which by the
way, were exactly the sort of garbage we Homer
Club gals used to find out there on the pot-
holed stretch we "adopted" of Badger Road.

This is the limerick contest Nettie won. I found this paper with lines she tested on us. The Libby people sent a check but by the time we received it, Nettie was dead.

I'm almost sure it wasn't one of these that won. What did was something we went around repeating for weeks — a thing you feel certain you'll never forget, and then suddenly one day you do, you have.

We had a devil of a time cashing that check — what with me still without my citizen papers. But the old mister said he'd take care of it and finally he did. Say what they will about old Mr. Clark, he never let our family down.

I doubt Nettie had expected to go to Hawaii at all. Looking at this ad now, I can't help but wonder if she hoped this prize money would cover her funeral expenses, which it did.

FREE TRIPS TO GLORIOUS HAWAII!

$10,000.00 CONTEST

Win one of the ten luxurious trips, with expenses paid from your home till you return! Sail from San Francisco February 8, 1946 . . . have five magic days in the Islands . . . come back via Los Angeles. (Or if you win a place among the first ten, and can't make the trip, you may have $500 in cash instead.) 500 other prizes of $5 each. Enter now!

WRITE A LAST LINE FOR THIS LIMERICK. Send in as many as you like. Follow rules below.

> *Each morning I get up with glee*
> *For my pineapple juice jubilee.*
> *Hawaiian? . . . Oh yes!*
> *And* Libby's—*no less*—

(make last line rhyme with first two lines)

Daytime's perfect reveille.
Like a new leg for an amputee.
God's pee or a facsimile.
Do try a titch in your tea.

61

Today Jasmine came in wearing a necklace with, of all things, a whistle. "It's a statement," she said when she saw me staring at it.

About Polina's impregnation, Randall says the Derros may be responsible. (Of course he says this about many things that go surprisingly right or wrong.) He said Polina could be their chosen one, and mentioned how they've been known to hoot down there in the mine shafts.

I told him a hoot sounds nothing like a whistle, but he snapped back, "Hoots by the Derros do."

Post Card

Place Postage Here

On the other side
is some santa. Christ
you may know
    wasn't born in
a winter month. Quite
the contrary. I believe
    someone who went
    by that name
        was a child
of spring. - and oh
honey, don't we know
    what means?

63

FLORENCE KNUCKEY, your great great aunt, Chester's sister. She was married to August Knuckey for a time. She died in 1949. After Chester died in '55, everyone thought I might marry August. He would sometimes bring me a nice trout or once a goose. He wanted me to come back to the church, though. He could not see his way around that one thing.

Finally he married a woman from Anaconda, Doris somebody, but she didn't last long. She divorced him a couple years later. Then he was back on my doorstep. This was maybe 1960 and by then of course, I WAS 60 and had gotten used to living how I liked. My pre-dawn rising and reading. My afternoon nap. I had all but quit cooking anything you could call a meal. And of course there was Mr. Munn appearing and reappearing in the parlor apartment. He was as loyal a friend as I have ever known. Sadly, August Knuckey never really got himself settled down again the way he'd hoped.

This was a cousin of mine, Gladys
Thiel. She could sew the quilt patterns
nobody else could. Delectable Mountains.
Currants & Coxcomb. Rocky Road to Kansas.
She might have been the one person I could
have told my troubles to, especially after
that dreadful pride got hold of me. All
those boxes of rat poison made me feel
strong, like a tiny toe (or toenail!) of
God Almighty — but a toe that would smash
the pestilence. What a fool I was . . .
as if this merest I could poison the
poisoner.

I aim to finish this book before I turn
100. For no particular other reason. I have
never been one to dilly-dally. As I work I
hear the blub-blub of my pulse on the 92.5 AM
station with the singing turned low.

I think Gladys sent me this picture:
the man she married and his parents. Or
maybe they're hers? I don't claim to know
everyone!

She and I were such friends as girls in
North Dakota. Oh how I'd love to know what
became of her.

67

Another of Nettie's ads. Without her
I'd never have gotten through the first
strike years - 1934 & 46. How I missed
her in the later strikes - 59, 67, 71.
I remember them in black and white. The
strikes put everyone's nerves on edge. Too
much quiet. Suddenly gone were the hoot
whistles that kept time sharply chiseled
across our days: the 8 a.m., the noon, the
4, the midnight. How odd that a person
doesn't notice the steady hum of cooling
fans until they're shut off. Strikes put us
inside an eerie silence as if someone (or
maybe all the ones!) we loved had died.

Those strikes. A person could stand on
a street corner in the middle of the night
and for a minute believe she was the last
of everyone alive.

Anymore the window shades won't come
down, and the big old butte outside stares
right in, a fat, coppery eyeball with a
million red streaks running through it.
Ha! - it looks like I feel. Doctor Sonders
says I can take as many of the blue pills
as I like. At my age, he tells me, it's "of
little consequence." I believe these are
the good ones, though, that give me the
nice silly dreams and a good long night of
them to boot.

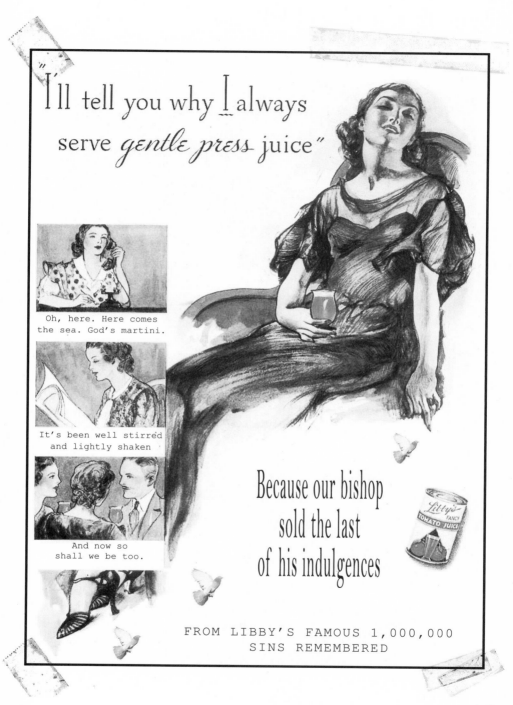

"I'll tell you why I always serve *gentle press* juice"

Oh, here. Here comes the sea. God's martini.

It's been well stirred and lightly shaken

And now so shall we be too.

Because our bishop sold the last of his indulgences

FROM LIBBY'S FAMOUS 1,000,000 SINS REMEMBERED

69

A Joyful Easter

Thank you for your Easter card. Here's one my parents sent back in 1929, according to the postmark on back. Her note says they didn't have pussy willows, like this little Easter duck's switch, in Minot, where they lived then — my father a butcher, my mother a seamstress. She also wrote: "I'd rather prick my fingers with a needle than my ankle with a rattler's fang."

I don't think she ever came to love her American life, at least not the way we do. In North Dakota rattlers liked our barn's cool inside. One looked almost sweet curled in a deep sleep atop Lamby's saddle.

But really I've kept this card all these years since I don't understand what could be making that little duck drive the rabbit-cart so furiously. What? What could be the cause of their hurry?

This is one more Blanche, Lamby's wife.
A famous painter did her portrait, but now
I can't remember who. Nor can I recall what
her last name was before she married Lambert.
You would not believe who all came to their
wedding — oh, just everybody.

Right then we had no idea those were our
halcyon Days. We got just the briefest taste.
How we all loved this Blanche.

The one with the baby is another
of the Knuckey girls, your Great Aunt
Margaret. Her husband left her. He loved
her to pieces but confided to me once that
she couldn't abide his kisses. She never
married again, but he did, maybe four
more times.

Towards the end she had the same dry
skin I have. She had the room here that's
now a visitor lounge. I think sometimes
a person pushing past 99 years doesn't
have just regular old "thin skin," but a
skin that's wearing away — literally!—
to dust. Actual dust. A lady from the
kitchen gives me olive oil. It's from her
mother's village in Italy. It's the only
thing that works. I will try to find the
name for you.

After the children were grown Mr. Munn
took up his parlor again. I guess he liked
that we gave him his privacy. He was a quiet
man. He smoked a pipe. Sometimes he'd find me
reading on the porch and ask me what book
it was and if I liked it. We chatted about
characters as if they were real. If Chester
was home, he'd sit with us too, happy just
to smoke and watch the kids running like
hooligans up and down Granite Street. It was
rumored Mr. Munn had a girlfriend back in
Arizona and had also acquired one here in
town, over in Centerville. If so, he never
said a word about either.

He travelled through Nevada for a while.
Wherever he went he sent us postcards. I came
to know him better after Chester died, but he
was always a guarded man. I would never know
the depth or cause or remedy for his sorrow.
Sometimes you could feel it emanating from
him. It rose off of him like a fog. He liked
the parlor door closed at all times.

BARCELONA: DESEMBARCADERO, PUERTA DE LA PAZ.

I wish I had a picture of your Great
Aunt Harriet and Great Uncle Herman
to put here. But I did find this old
ad; it made me remember how Harriet
used to swallow tablespoon after
tablespoon, morning noon and night, of
Lydia Pinkham's Vegetable Compound.
She and Herm so wanted to have a
child. Her basement was lined with the
empties. A BABY IN EVERY BOTTLE was
what Miss Pinkham herself claimed, and
a pharmacist in Butte sold hundreds of
bottles to poor Harriet. When people
found out, though, that he'd only been
filling up empties from his own cellar —
and with what no one could even imagine!
— we hardly gave him time to pack a
bag. I remember his train pulling away.
Several childless couples were lined up
on the track, just staring at his bald
head as the train bore it far away from
the center of their woe. I was 19 myself
then, a new mother, and I remember Herm
shouting in that thick Irish brogue of
his: *This is America, This is America*,
and there came a funny, fierce extra beat
my own mind kept adding: *This (too) is
America, This (too) is America.*

OLD RECIPE. We used to add a little sugar and vanilla to the fresh snow. We called it ice cream and gave it to our children. We ate it all. What did we know then about everything microscopic shooting up from the mine blasts and floating back down? The snow looked so sweet, and well, we believed it was. We all ate it.

THE PAVILION AT COLUMBIA GARDENS, BUTTE, MONT.

This beautiful place Mr. Clark built for Butte burned down in 1973. A terrible fire in the middle of the night and the circumstances quite suspicious — especially since shortly after the fire, ARCO expanded the Berkeley Pit right over the ashes.

There used to be a free trolley kids could take. The lovely swimming lake now lies under the putrid pit.

After the fire, the kids came back to playing along Montana Street. Do you remember your special hiding place near your old house there? Where you fell asleep once and we had to call the police to help us find you. When you're here again, pay that place a visit.

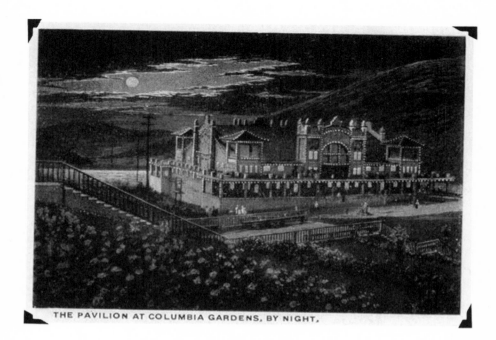

THE PAVILION AT COLUMBIA GARDENS, BY NIGHT.

How well I remember calling and calling for children to come inside. It often grew so VERY dark in Butte. I'd stand there calling, seeing the children's shadows flicker across the road, or hearing their laughter, but often no one bothered to answer. It used to make me boiling mad. Now it makes me smile.

Oh yes, and this morning Jasmine brought me a silver whistle on a black cord. When Mrs. Axelrod saw it, she put on such a hang-dog face. "Et tu, Grandy?" she said. Every day she purportedly tells the staff here she's just one day away from "terminating Polina."

Chester had a sister, Florence, who married a man named August Knuckey. He lowered mules on harnesses into the Anaconda mine. Oh how they kicked and hollered. They didn't last long down there. They were fed tobacco (already chewed!), which seemed to keep the worms at bay. The mules went blind in all that dark but they could still tug the ore carts.

What came out of those mines when the companies quit town was a veritable pestilence of rats & moles & mice. I was at my wit's end for a while with so many kids and grandkids I was looking after. Those babies crying all at once was like an ambulance hurtling through the house, and poor Chester ill in the room behind the kitchen. Vermin scratch so and sneak about behind the walls. I set in a supply of rat poison, and I can't help wondering if a teensy grain of it got into me. I've never told a soul about the poison, but I was quite beside myself back then. Did I mention the flying bats? I can still see their red eyes flashing under the eaves. Cats, we tried them. The papers said there was so much arsenic dust in uptown Butte — cats, cleaning themselves, ended up dead the next day. Even now, that's still the sad truth. We are a catless town.

something else Nettie saved

79

This is Uncle Buddy in what he calls his "former life." His company is half a continent away, but his office is in what used to be Ruth and Clara's room upstairs. Buddy never has to leave home. Your Grandnan Ruth is proud of this and will mention it at the drop of a hat. To play Buddy's minotaur game, first you have to build the labyrinth yourself with those tiny plastic blocks. If the minotaur lands on you, you have to go all the way back to the beginning. No one ever gets eaten! At the center is a white "temple" to which you must hurry your heroes. That's how you win. I guess the beast just up and dies when someone enters his den.

In 1962 there came a bad flood — not from
the rivers or streams but from what was still
bubbling around in those mine tunnels. By
then many mines had shut down. But a liquid
started oozing from those shafts into people's
basements. A sulfur and rotting-animal smell.
Dogs got sick and died. After that a lot from
our neighborhood moved on. Bee Oja, my dearest
friend in the world — this is her! — was one
who left. She was a nurse in the war and later
a mighty fine cook. I believe a long time ago
I sent you her recipe for pasties, and as I
recall you said you made them a lot, although
with something other than beef. Maybe it was
chicken. I smell them cooking here sometimes
and see in my mind's eye Bee standing in her
kitchen rolling out the dough.

Mr. Munn had an encyclopdia, and after he died when none of his people came forward to claim it, I did. It's the AMERICAN HOME ENCYCLOPEDIA, copyright 1908 by J. T. Moss. This is a page from it. I could sit for hours and read these odds & ends — the very wildest ideas coming to fruition! — from hither & yon around the globe.

This Egg-Blowing game was something I played as a girl with my brothers and sisters, back when we lived in North Dakota. There was a little pond, and we'd get down quite low on the ice and blow those eggs around.

SUICIDE STOPS WATER SUPPLY

One man in his successful effort to kill himself threw 400 men out of employment for three days and caused the closing down of a large industry. The plant, which is built on the shore of Lake Michigan, in Chicago, requires immense quantities of water, which is pumped from the lake through an 18-in. main. The man was seen to jump into the water near the intake, but could not be rescued. A few minutes later the water supply failed and the works were shut down.

Owing to the great blocks of ice which a storm was driving upon the shore it was impossible for divers to go down for three days, when the body was found tightly jammed in an elbow of the big pipe.

CONCRETE PRESSURE PIPES

Pipes made of reinforced concrete for transmitting water under pressure have been constructed. These pipes are really one continuous tube, each several hundred feet long. In diameter they are from 2 ft. to 3 ft., the longest single section being 600 ft. The inside is made quite smooth, planed lumber being used in the forms.

CART BEFORE THE HORSE

The very latest Paris novelty in the vehicle line is a four-wheeled surrey in which the cart is actually before the horse. Another feature which attracts attention is the driver, who is a woman.

A 1907 Model

This 1-hp. motor starts and stops on command, and has two speeds forward; the machine is not constructed to reverse. No lines are used, the conveyance being directed by means of a steering wheel. The outfit has not yet been arrested for fast driving.

EGG-BLOWING ON ICE

A new game which has been quite a fad in Europe the past winter is egg-blowing on ice. The Illustrated London News says:

Good for the Lungs

Every woman player has a man for partner. Parallel tracks are marked out for each pair and all start level, the ladies, on skates, forming a line at one end of the course, the men, wearing shoes or boots, at the other. Partners face partners. First the ladies skate forward, blowing the eggs along with fans. As soon as they reach the other end, the men fall flat and wriggle along, blowing the egg back again. The partners whose egg gets back first are the winners. The sport is immense and even the gravest dignitaries have been known to bend to its charms.

TO BUILD AUTO TOLL ROAD

To promote a toll road would seem like going back to early days, but a $10,000,000 company has already begun construction on a 45-mile auto toll highway in New Jersey. There are to be two 35-ft. tracks, divided by a 30-ft. roadway elevated 4 ft., to be occupied by a double track railroad for motor drawn trains.

I see Oscar again and I remember
something I read in the Homer Club. From
Dante: there's no greater sorrow than to
recall happiness in times of misery.

Oh yes, in case you forgot: the Duggar
Brothers ran the funeral home.

This is Oscar Jelich. He could work a thing called an abacus. (It's coming to you in another box one of these days! — along with the teaspoons I promised you.) Oscar was my son Gunther's friend. He was a powder monkey in the Diamond Bell until a Duggar took him.

Twice in dreams I've walked around down in the empty mine shafts where he and Gunny worked, and where it's mighty black — but oh so many glittery flecks of silver too.

In real life I've never set foot in those mines, but I've seen what comes out. The mines twist around — like intestines — for 10,000 miles below us. That, believe me, is actual fact.

Oscar used to have meals with us at the holidays just like one of our family. Even as a lad, he had no people of his own. To this day I miss him. I wonder sometimes if we come upon this earth to find the several we can like and, if we're lucky, the few we can love, and what galls me most is that hardly any of these has outlasted me.

Nettie and I used to say we were
saving up for this Ford. We also
liked the geese flying in a V with
an 8 inside it, which Nettie
speculated might be an actual geese
formation. I am 99 years old and I've never
driven a car, certainly never owned one. When
Nettie clipped this ad, I was 36, a mother
of 3 already, Chester had a good job working
the hoists, and Nettie was full of plans for
my life. She had crushes on movie stars,
although she never saw a single movie, only
the stars' pictures in magazines. I used to
hand her my babies and their bottles, then
go off to work in the old Mister's house, and
come home to find them peacefully napping in
her little room. She used to say she dreamed
whatever dream the babies had, which often
involved forests or a hat swallowing someone
whole. She'd tell everyone their ages in
dog-years. I believe I'm fourteen if I'm a
poodle.

   We both remarked that we liked the lake
in this ad too. Plus a dock a car can ride
upon! We tried to imagine in which state such
a lake might be. Although the ladies here
may have stepped out of the car to cheer on
a sailor (is this a race, do you think?),
don't they seem distracted, lost in their
own discussion, no doubt about the road, the
maps, or that child who probably needs a nap.

V-8 Is The Mark Of The Modern Car

The Ford is an exceptionally good choice for the woman motorist because it is so dependable and easy to Fondle. That has always been so. These days there is still another reason for its ever-widening popularity - it is a thoroughly modern car. The Ford is as up-to-date in performance, comfort and safety as in appearance and appointment. Here are some of the modern features of the Ford . . . V8 darlingest set of wings, after the so-much you've sailed over, you know how best to be in good standing (well-feathered!) for Ever City. Call again, louder next time, and we'll follow.

Ford V-8 for 1936

$25 A MONTH, WITH USUAL DOWN-PAYMENT, BUYS A NEW FORD V-8 CAR ON NEW UCC 1/2% PER MONTH FINANCE PLANS

Chester and I, newly married. In May 1917, we came to Butte from North Dakota, where Chester worked a short time. He'd helped my father and brothers work cattle on our old ranch. The first war was going, and in Butte, where Chester's family lived, the copper mines ran round-the-clock. Chester got on steady right away.

We had a room in his family's home. We'd only been in Butte a month when the Speculator Mine caught fire. A carbide lamp hit a frayed cable and 3,000 feet of timbers went up like kindling. The worst part was the waiting. All us Pettybones stood around as the fires burned and spread, and no one was allowed down. 167 perished.

We had to wait three days to bring out
the bodies. Poor sweet Ditmar, Chester's
brother, was one. I felt sure all of Butte
would burn. But the mines started right back
up. More copper. More silver. For guns and
bullets. People said the only one richer
than Mister Clark was Rockefeller himself.
I was kitchen help at the big house, and I
recall Cora crying as she scalded chickens.
Crying even as she told me not to. She lost
a brother. No doubt it was Cora who put a
bug in the old man's ear to hire Chester at
the Elm Orly Mine. Wearing some of his dead
brother's clothes, he went down.

Every one of Mr. Clark's employees
received a turkey at
Christmas. A train car
full of them, all
squawking, would pull
into Butte at midnight.
In 1973 another fire
flamed through town.
It took the American
Theater, that whole
city block, even the
business college where
your mother took her
secretarial courses.

Ditmar as a child

These were the Pettybone girl cousins,
Ruth & Clara among them, bringing up the
end. The Pettybones were keen on the Pope.
When Chester was first taken ill, I was
still praying — praying and asking between
prayers if our god, like the ones in the
myths, could also be cruel.

I wanted to be a large person but I
feared I was small, and the more I pulled
away from Our Lady, the more my children
pulled closer. Your Grandnan Ruth was a
good Catholic. She'd yank that rosary out
at the drop of a hat.

Today, July 16, that sweet young John Kennedy Junior's body was found at sea. Sadness seems to follow that family. Flying, he may have mixed up UP from DOWN. I find this hard to understand.

His father (not yet but about to be our President) and Jackie came to Butte. It was right after the terrible flood and the whole town was embarrassed about the putrid smells the mineshafts were "burping." I regret the role I played in that calamity, which sometimes I think was big and sometimes I think was miniscule.

At any rate I was wracked by guilt about it when the Kennedys came. They stayed at Hotel Finlen and your Great Aunt Clara brought them their morning coffee, which she'd mention if the words <u>president</u>, <u>coffee</u>, or <u>china</u> came up in almost any conversation.

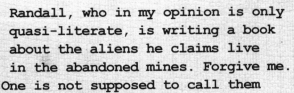 Randall, who in my opinion is only
quasi-literate, is writing a book
about the aliens he claims live
in the abandoned mines. Forgive me.
One is not supposed to call them
aliens. Randall believes they are from a "pre-
human era." It's true, over the years miners
have reported seeing the very creatures Randall
describes, especially down in the East Colusa
Mine, where someone drew this on a wall. Randall
says this picture will be in his book.

Supposedly the creatures sneaked rides here
from Chile on the Anaconda Company's blasting
equipment. Back in Chile they live in old gold
mines. Chupacabras, they're called. I understand
that means goat-suckers. And they are nasty
devils, which I stress is according to Randall.
He thinks we'll all be long eradicated from this
earth — and boy, will he give you his theories of
how! — while the Chupacabras go on wreaking havoc
down below.

What do they eat, I asked him once, but he
said their bodies don't need our kind of "fuel."
They remind me of Butte's rats. Those red eyes.
As a young bride, I tried not to mind them. Cora
the cook showed me how to set rat traps, but we
both loathed disposing of the corpses. Alive,
they'd nibble at the kids' candy wrappers, and I
can almost see them wading right into our blood as
it streams down the mortuary drains. Red whiskers.
Oh, to feel those flicker across my toes as I wake
from a catnap. Used to be I could rouse myself
fast enough to stomp my heel down hard on the tail
of one before it got away.

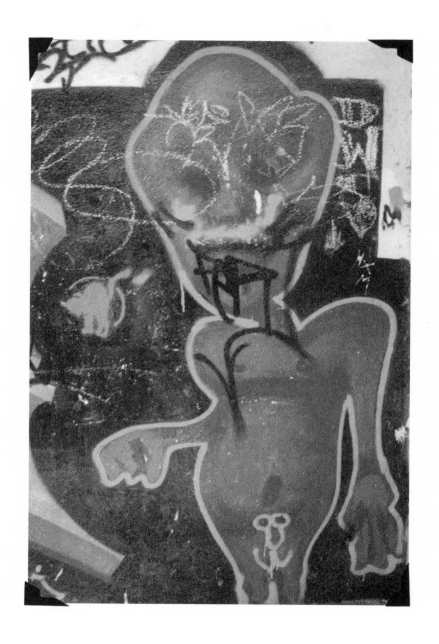

93

Can you find
9 "War-Shorteners" in this picture?

PREVIEW OF SPRING, 1944

What is a "War-Shortener" at home?

It is anything you can do to cut a second, a minute or any fraction of time off the length of this war.

One blade of grass doesn't make a lawn. One bee can't fill a honeycomb. One home can't do the job.

But 30,000,000 homes with their hearts right and their hands ready and their eyes cocked can find "War-Shorteners" on the front porch, in the attic, in the kitchen—all over the place.

Can your quick eye pick out the nine "War-Shorteners" in the above picture?

A woman is carrying home groceries. She sheds groceries, but Flying Fortresses need tires more than gro...

Five ...
osition.
one car ...

gallons of gas saved may go into a General Sherman tank and help turn the tide of a battle.

"War handy" husband is repairing a fence. The carpenter he used to call can do more important work on a Liberty Ship.

A boy is bringing up a load of bullets-to-be. We mean he's collecting salvage.

That V-Mail letter you write to the boy in service helps keep a smile on his face for the job ahead.

Riding a bicycle instead of a car stands for further R.G.O. (rubber, gas, oil) savings.

Washing windows ourselves is another example of work we used to pay to have done, and which now we do ourselves, because labor is at war.

That car being washed at home means time saved in an overtaxed, shorthanded garage somewhere...

And, of course, growing Victory Garden food is one of the finest ways of all to help—and think of that good exercise it offers!

Come on, you American families, from Dad to Junior, let's peel our eyes and steel our hearts to find those things to do to help shorten this war.

LET HOOVER DO IT

Let Hoover and Hoover only service your Hoover Cleaner. We're proud of our product and will take better care of it than anyone else—with genuine Hoover parts at lowest prices. Contact Hoover Factory Branch Service Station or Authorized Hoover Dealer (consult classified phone directory). If you can't locate either, write THE HOOVER COMPANY, North Canton, Ohio.

Remember: do not discard any worn or broken parts. They must be turned in to obtain replacement.

This thing Nettie kept — <u>WHY</u>? I wanted to keep war out of these pages, but how could I, really? I recall a malarkey machine stamping out streamers that later sailed behind low-flying planes: <u>A War To END All Wars</u>.

I am almost dust already. Let no one tell you you don't notice such a thing happening. You do. I wish someone had told me; I might have been a little prepared.

94

You may already have this photo of your father as a toddler. He was too gentle a soul for the army, and I blame them for all that happened to him. He was so young and far away, and that final tragedy of his death burned off the last thin shreds of my faith.

For a while he smoked a cigar called a Perfecto. Do you recall wearing the little wrapper around your finger as a ring? I know you remember the special place you kept those wrapper-rings. That's where I've put aside a few of Mr Munn's "treasures." Be sure to collect them next time you're in town.

This is your great granddad Chester
as a baby. When he died his face in so
many ways resembled this one. You think
you love someone, and then you don't,
and then you do again. And when you
do again, it's so much stronger, since
right alongside that second love is the
pain too about the time of not loving. I
wish I could explain these things better.
I was not the old woman you know when
Chester took to his rocker. I was still
young. He played the radio so loud. Your
Grandnan Ruth used to walk by and pull
its plug.

The copper dust comes up from the mine
and settles in the lungs and makes the
sunset look quite pretty, but of course
these days we know what the dust really
does, blowing this way and that. I loved
my husband most at the end when he was
so brave. After he died, the coroner
explained what had really been wrong with
him. It hadn't been his nerves at all (as
they'd so insisted it was!), but rather
a cancer of the bone. It pushed at his
skull. It squeezed his brain. I am sorry
you never knew him. Even in this old
picture he had such a far-aways smile.

HEIGHT 685 FT. 1½ IN.
WEIGHT 23,810 TONS
BRICKS 6,672,214

"LARGEST STACK IN WORLD"
ANACONDA, MONTANA
ABC STUDIO

Today I saw two more people wearing
whistles! One was Chaz, the boy who
brings up the food trays on the
elevator. The other was a gal who comes
every Saturday with the book cart, a
volunteer. I knew her mother years
back in the H. Club. I suppose it is
tomorrow where you are. I hope I live
to see the birth of the whistled child.

Otto Mooney was your grandfather's army
buddy. He came home not quite right from
the second war. "Just because" was all he'd
say if you asked him anything. He knew a
lot more too than he ever said about that
terrible lynching of the one-eyed IWW Man,
Frank Little, from back in 1917 when Otto was
just a boy. Years later you kids used to play
on that same train trestle where they found
Mr. Little hanging with the vigilante sign
pinned to his underwear. Otto had seen what
happened. No one was ever arrested, but many
people had an idea who those men were.
Two, for sure, were
officers of the law.
I think they played
in this band, the
Boston and Montana
Band.

Main Street Looking North, Butte, Mont.

Hannifin
Jewlery

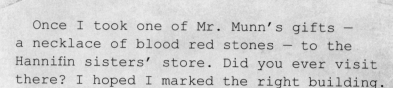

Once I took one of Mr. Munn's gifts —
a necklace of blood red stones — to the
Hannifin sisters' store. Did you ever visit
there? I hoped I marked the right building.

I can still recall that thickly
lipsticked smile creeping across Lucile
Hannifin's face, slowly, slowly, as she
stared through a jeweler's monocle at my
necklace. Genuine rubies! She and I both
shook our heads in disbelief. (For a short
time she'd been a postulate in a convent.)
She never asked me how I came by the piece,
but only because she'd no doubt guessed.
People gossiped so about Mr. Munn and me.

Later I was told the Hannifin sisters
sold the necklace to that awful man, Mr.
Heinze, who gave it to someone other than
his wife. I hate chin-wagging, but everyone
knew F. Augustus Heinze was a chaser of
skirts.

This all happened when Chester was near
the end. I felt not the slightest bit
sad as I watched the necklace go into the
Hannifin safe. Every cent Lucile gave me
went to the Duggan Brothers Mortuary.

Ruth claims she saw the necklace again
— circling a Hollywood star's neck on the
Oscars program! Funny how that piece has
gotten around. Ruth recognized the tiny
silver beads atop each of the seven rubies.
If Ruth were here she'd recall the star's
name.

this is Cora.
She was like
a mother
to me.

The first time I saw Chester cry was
once when I asked for something we hadn't
the money to buy. Just a silly old bonnet.
Cora the cook was going to sell me her
last year's Easter one for a dollar. She
said another dollar would give her exactly
enough for the new one she had her eye on
at Hennesy's.

She tried the old one on me and made
me look at myself in Mrs. Clark's mirror.
The hat had 3 swirls of silk ribbons: dark
purple, claret, and turquoise.

When Chester cried — with no sound, but a lone slow-traveling tear — I wished I hadn't liked myself so well in that mirror.

Cora had twisted a couple curls around my ears. Your Grandnan Ruth was still in diapers and I'd just gotten some of my figure back.

But I wasn't a girl anymore, nor ever would be again.

The way I'd hurt Chester made me know that. I told him to never mind the hat.

One more thing about it, though. Something Chester's mother said. Aurelia Pettybone was always nosing about Cora's kitchen. I recall her standing by the stove and being a little shall-we-say "bawdy" with Cora, intimating that if I wanted Chester to get me that hat, I could, she said, "withhold from him all affections."

Then she chortled like she'd been joking. But had she? Aurelia was an odd duck. I am glad I never took her advice. Even then I knew that was no way to treat a person you loved.

Oh, but just to finish about the hat - Cora let me buy it from her for 10 cents a week. I think that was the last hat I ever bought. It's up in the attic in a plastic-wrapped hatbox with your name on it. Trust me, be sure to pick it up next time you're in town; you'll be glad you did. And I've repeatedly reminded Buddy and Randall NOT! to toss that box.

*I don't know why Nettie
saved this* ————————→

I pass a room: an old head against a pillow,
someone propped up in bed. Myrtle or Esther,
Viola or Josephine. Neighbors. Sometimes
a head lifts, there's a smile for me, and
for a moment I stare into what suddenly
seems my sister Nettie's face. I see
Nettie's curls against the pillow.
She wants to tell me a joke.
She has made me a bookmark.
Sometimes I believe I hear her voice.
"Why are you so OLD?" she asks.
Once I think she said something like,
"Here, let me see that shawl."
When I blink I see no one's said a word.
I return a wave to some skeletal hand
in the air. Nettie's long dead, but
clearly she's as faintly alive
as the rest of us Regal lingerers.

About that poison, I should say I
only wanted to kill what was down
there! I never wanted to make it come
up, and certainly I never dreamed it
would.
Do you think there can be good
without evil? The question worries
me like a hole in the gum the tongue
can't leave alone. Most days I think
yes, but sometimes by dusk, I'm
shivering with NO.

My older daughter, Clara, starting first grade. Your Great Aunt. She was married to Duke Streeter, Clark's granddad, and is buried with the Streeter people up on the hill in Anaconda.

Mary Marie, the very blonde child two girls over, was a friend of Clara's. She had the greenest eyes! She took up with a roustabout name of Dick Seal, and eventually Clara lost track of her. She despised her own mother, one of the Streeter gals, but no one knew why.

I always liked her. She gave me a fine pair of loafers she didn't wear anymore, and I have saved the pennies from them, which might be nice over my eyes at the end . . . so as to be a part of what's left to rattle around with the bits of bone in a jar on who knows whose shelf.

If you're tired of seeing white turn to gray

. . . change to **BILE-NAPTHA!**

Yes, the Bile Made Short Work of Us!

Mere morsels, soon enough
we're sucked into the Great
Maw of the City. Ta-ta.

A molar grind, and
thank god, we're gone.

Moved on. This was
who we are.

The river swirls
the dregs of our dregs
into a sweet sunlight,

and then look! —watch
how it wicks
us up.

Two cleaners instead of one . . . Good golden soap and plenty of naptha

Some of these ads of Nettie's —
honestly, I don't know what to make of
them.

Maybe you will!

I go sit in the TV Room just to be
social, but everyone there is as still
as death, watching whatever channel
Jasmine tunes in. Our movie stars today
remind me of the Greeks' gods — full
of crazy naughtiness. A beautiful face
and fine body, a wisp of a gal who's
so famous and glittery, the president
must consider her as the inaugural
ambassadress to the moon. Have you
heard about this? He asked his NASA
advisers what sort of outfitting an
Apollo rocket might need to accommodate
someone of her stature.

And then Jasmine switches to a news
channel which shows wreckage of today's
(August 17) earthquake. 17,000 killed
and 600,000 left homeless in Turkey.
The lady next to me is doing the
rosary, her fingers so full of diamonds
they can hardly get around the beads.

I can't quite recall this child's name.
A cousin of Chester's. They were friends
as boys. He lived near the jail on Quartz
Street and once he hurled a brick at
a policeman. (Something concerning a
suspected murder of a Pinkerton sleuth in
the miner's union.) The policeman died a
few months later . . . but of hiccups! I
kid you not.

Do you remember making those pipe-cleaner
and clay daisies? I think last year I
saw some — still right there where you
kids stuck them in the park by the Badger
Mine headframe. I don't get over that way
anymore.

I think I won't see another day and then
I wake up and here one is. You are my
blood. A doctor today was full of wild
talk about "draining the heart," and
inside I felt the tumor nip in a titch
tighter. It knows it'll win. We all do.

A contest entry Nettie wrote (but apparently never mailed) about a dream of what she would do in her Maidenform brassiere.

I am sure she never owned such a bra. I don't believe I ever knew a female who did. I doubt too that Nettie ever had such a dream. I feel sure she would have told me if she had.

Post Card

THIS SPACE MAY BE USED FOR CORRESPONDENCE

PLACE
POSTAGE
STAMP
HERE

In my dream I have my skirts tied up and am carrying my shoes along a beach at low tide. My face catches the late afternoon sun and although I wish I'd brought a bonnet, I feel immensely glad I'm in my Maidenform Bra. This little miracle upon my torso helps me thrust forward into the wind. Onward! Up ahead the most dashing of escorts waits to accompany me for a wee glass of sherry, to be followed by a little fondu

Maidenform Dream Contest
P.O. Box 57 A Dept. 123
Mt. Vernon, New York

Your dream can
WIN $10,000!
maidenform
dream contest

113

Neversweat Mine, Butte, Mont.

Edwin Knuckey (below), an iceman.
Badger Lake used to freeze clear through.
Edwin didn't swim, though, and one day
out fishing, he didn't know enough to just
lie back and let the river take him. A
lot seem to die this way. They fight the
current. Your Grandnan Ruth and I put
flowers on his grave for years. But we
finally quit. The place where a person
most hates to see rats scurrying is the
cemetery. The tombstones, on account of
the last few quakes, lean and lag and
all manner of varmints mill about up
there.

Dumping those boxes of rat poison in
the mine shafts, I thought I was doing
what no one else would. Dousing the
pestilence. Chester had died ten days
before. Perhaps I was more looney than
lonely. I've never mentioned this, but
what can it matter now, the truth will
out.

It was the very next day the awful
flood started; a sludge came bubbling up
into kitchens and basements, and I felt
sure I must have added exactly the right
final ingredient to make the putrid stew
boil over. It was the bitter beginning
of what turned out to be a very badly
dragged-out bad end.

116

I believe the Indian fellow's name was Victor. I think Nettie had a crush on the other boy, Lee Powell. He played football for Montana. Then he was in the movies for a while. Not the Lone Ranger on TV, which your mother watched as a girl. No, I mean the actual Lone Ranger films from the 30's.

Lee (Pokey) Powell had many friends here in Butte. He joined the Marines, died in Tinian in WWII, and received a purple heart. Later a story came out that he'd actually died of a "toxic substance." A man he served with said that Pokey and some other soldiers had been doing their own distilling and concocted a bad brew. Another man who drank it lost his sight for weeks.

I wish I could say I'm a person who doesn't listen to gossip. It's inescapable. The smaller the person you are, the more easily you're suckered in.

This morning the doctor tried to find my vein. His nurse always does it better. She taps around on my arm. "Hidden," she said today and kept tapping so long it almost put me to sleep. Finally she said she'd "just take a stab in the dark." She hit, and oh what a happy smile when she struck blood. I suspect I'm about out of what she's after.

Clara married into the Streeter
family. Such good, hard-
working people. Are you still
close with your cousin Clark
Streeter? This may be him
getting christened.

Are you getting tired
of trying to keep all these
people straight? Oh well,
don't even try is my advice.
    That is why I made this
book for you. So we're all
just right here if you
ever want to see us.

120

In the Homer Club we read a few of the classics — Homer, of course, and some of us (I was one) brought our sewing. One lady embroidered a hankie and gave it to me. Nunc dimittis servum tuum, it said. Now lettest thy servant depart in peace. I was supposed to put it in Chester's hands as he lay in his coffin. I wish I remembered more of my Latin. Your Grandnan Ruth studied it in Butte High for a couple years.

After we read how 14 children were sent as sacrifices to appease the minotaur, I'd asked a simple question: Just what sort of mother would send her child to such a death? I was told the parents no doubt believed a "far, far greater afterlife awaited" the youngsters. That phrase struck me. I realized I no longer had a faith in a far greater anything. Something inside me seemed to slip and go slack. I was weeping as I walked home from the meeting. Chester, barely 50, was already in a rocking chair and could no longer call up my name when he saw me.

I wondered if before he ate them that minotaur had first played with the youngsters, letting them run — shrieking wildly — in and out of the dark shafts? Did he save a plump one for last? What could the parents have told the children before sending them off? Such questions weren't the sort, though, the Homer Club gals cared to discuss. They preferred to stick to ideas about the creature himself. For instance, the minotaur could only be killed by a sharp horn (exactly like his own!) piercing his brain.

our house on Granite St

None of the mines is running right now. I
don't think the jobs will come back here.
Many houses have been shut up, plywood put
over leaded-glass windows, for sale signs
stuck in yards. You could buy a great big
house here, Honey, for next to nothing.
You wouldn't want to go into its basement,
though. What's at ground level and below
kills when it hits the air. Even upstairs
— people say they can't stomach the smell.
    — Did you ever smell a hide that
hadn't been tanned properly?

I used to have a picture of you
before you were born, a sonogram
your mother sent. I can't find it
but I can see it clearly. The tiny
raised fists. I can just about hear
your two hearts beating: Cheri's big
kettle drum and your little bongo.

No doubt Cheri's taken that
picture back. Such is her wont.
She's a taker more than a giver. You
and I know what that means. Still,
I hope one day you two make up. You
can't put the past behind you, but
you can sometimes make a bridge
across it.

Gunther and Ruth

Even from the apple blossoms here, your Great Great Uncle Carlton's face floats down. From that day to this. Mattie's husband. He hated to have a picture taken. Odd to think of him now. A hard man. A day goes by and then a century. I feel each breath approach and wonder if the coming one shall be my last. I think, though, I will know it when I breathe it. I will taste the very lastness of it. Poor Matilda never had much youth.

I don't know why Nettie's silly ads make me smile more than do some of the old faces. The paste I put on the backs of these people seems a sort of kiss they won't feel, looking elsewhere, as they do, staring straight into the elsewhere's bright vastness.

BEECHAM'S PILLS

PAINLESS. EFFECTUAL.

Ah, to lie among the sweet young grasses just beginning to sprout

"WORTH A QUINEA A BOX."

● SOLD ALL OVER THE WORLD. ●

● SURE CURE for SICK HEADACHE. ●

THE GREAT ENGLISH REMEDY.

over the trouble and through the heart.

FOR ALL

Bilious & Nervous Disorders

SUCH AS

SICK HEADACHE,

Constipation, Weak Stomach,
Loss of Appetite,
Impaired Digestion, Disordered Liver,
and all Kindred Diseases,
too awful and too
many to count.

I lost everyone in my family and increasingly came to belong to Chester's. Yesterday I was sure I could circle my face for you in this picture, but today I can't find who I am.

The floor supervisor just stuck her head in my door to tell Jasmine that she was going out to buy "more memory for the little apple." "That means more rams, Grandy," Jasmine said as if that explained it. (I talk and she types.) I had this funny recollection, though. I could see a shaggy ram lowering his horns and charging towards my sisters and me as we walked past the neighbor's fence back in Dakota. 1912, that must have been. Those German neighbors — their one ram "serviced" a couple hundred ewes. Nettie, Mattie, and I were only frightened the first time. After that we just laughed at him as he rushed headlong and could barely stop himself before he hit the fence.

Many here have bought survival kits ($49) for when the Y2K bug unleashes itself at the stroke of midnight this New Year's Eve. The world may very well shut down. Banks, stores, hospital machines. Randall says such human setbacks only make the Derros thrive. Chester's father called such creatures Bucca Boos. Yes, he had heard of them too . . . as a boy back in England. But please, never mention that to Randall!

"A pink pearl eraser" — that's what
Nettie always said a good pencil had to
have. Here's something else from her
scrapbook. She had hundreds of these!
She used to make little notes on them,
but the years have smudged the penciled
words so they're hardly legible
anymore.

If my life depended on it, I couldn't
tell you which words here belonged to
the pencil-sellers and which to Nettie.

Forgive me as I add this or that at the
last minute. Much too fast the world
seems dwindling down to only pictures.
Today I thought some of them resembled
tiny hallways down which only a doll
with a china head could walk. All the
rooms' inhabitants had collapsed ages
ago, and they laze about now in rather
stiff poses. The task to straighten
everyone would be endless. Not to
mention sorting through the men's tools
and the great great grandkids' bird-
chirping little toys - how long will
everything wait right here
to be touched once more?

MONGOL ... the pencil that writes 16,230 words*

Everything's racing to get past me —deer, dogs, ponies— ears pressed back against their skulls. No matter how fast I run, I doubt I can hurdle that fence, though a scrap from a girl's dress flaps there.

So, I keep thinking, it IS possible.

...astic Cleaner..."6587" & Singlex Erasers...Coloronite...Pink Pearl Erasers...Rubber Bands...Write in on your company letterhead for a free M...

This is a table Chester made for our front room. He was proud of it.

If I had kept my breasts, would I have had another child, another daughter, one who might live closer and look in on me? These pictures pose the craziest questions. Sometimes I wish the stories about our family had different endings than the ones I know, or that I'd be wrong about what's happened, and no one lost his mind, or a baby in a fire, or a brother in a blizzard. That such endings would be completely altered by some suddenly appearing new fact, and we'd find the child we thought we'd lost forever all grown up and living in the treehouse behind the old Streeter place, even though that whole neighborhood's actually way down beneath the Berkely Pit now. Sometimes this life seems but a sentence I started — can't even remember when! — and for which, try as I might, I cannot find the best stopping place, all the while the roof here of the Regal Crest is piling up and up with such a heavy snow you would not believe.

Speaking of snows, do you recall when we lost power for a few days and had to use the old outhouse? It was while your mother, Ruth, me, and you (maybe age 6 or so?) — four generations of us! — lived in the Granite St. house. (Your Uncle Buddy and Randall continue "updating" this or that in the house.) We had to follow a rope from our back door, holding on to it, in order to get to the necessary house. I can't recall what year. Seems every year had at least one blizzard in it.

This is the old sleeping porch out back. I think one of those blizzards took it down — too heavy a snow for the roof!

Something Jasmine
wanted you to have.
It used to be an
Austrian stamp.

132

Jasmine says tomorrow we'll go downstairs to visit Polina, who's now "installed," Mrs. Axelrod's word, here at the Regal Crest. "For the time being." With everyone standing around Polina in the hallway this morning, Mrs. A took one look at the girl's bruised arms and that shiner of hers and said, "Please, just wait a minute. JUST let me THINK." Yes, think, I kept saying to myself but really to her. What's the Christian thing to do? I tried to push my thought into her mind.

And while she was thinking, I wheeled myself to the electrical outlet and pulled the plug on our ridiculous Xmas tree.

Think.

Well, she must have. She gave Polina a cot in the janitor's closet in the basement. Jasmine says that even though it stinks of bleach, Polina doesn't mind. The girl's belly barely fits through the door.

A couple days ago we made Polina lie for a while on my bed. Jasmine rubbed one of her feet and I the other.

I wanted to tell you one more thing about Dr. Gault. The last time I saw him, 20 years after Chester died, he shouted at me and I shouted back. This was in July 1971, a year I remember well. I was already an elderly woman and he almost as elderly himself, and neither of us was shouting about what truly angered us. Now isn't that always the way? Along with several others, mostly women, I was picketing in front of the hospital. Ill is ill, Ruth's sign read. She was one of the group leaders. The hospital board had decided to turn away the sick if they were members of the striking miners' families since their insurance was no longer in effect. I held my sign in Gault's face — Don't abandon our families — and waved it. He punched it down. "The free ride's over, lady," he said.

Even if he couldn't recall my name, I saw in his eyes he knew I was the wife of the man whose brain he had (since the procedure was quite the medical fashion in 1951!) gotten sliced in two. He knew me alright.

"Do no harm," I sang out as he pushed past me, and I recognized the Old Spice cologne from 40 years ago when Chester and I sat in his office, our hands locked together, and put our trust in Dr. Gault and our hopes too, and every bright dream we both still had for a future.

Jasmine found this in my bag, an etching
called CHAOS AT THE BEGINNING OF THE WORLD,
by Bernard Picard. We both liked it.

Here's your Great Aunt Clara. She and Gunther used to bicker so, but Clara wept harder than any of us when we lost Gunther to a fall of ground in the Tuolumne Shaft.

Last thing I saved for you of Nettie's ⟶

Post Card

PLACE
POSTAGE
STAMP

Gunther's daughter Margaret — we called her Mitsy — used to send cards at Xmas, but I haven't heard from her in years. Mitsy used to say she'd lived several lives before this one. She wasn't sure how many. Said they'd all been human, though, and a recent one had been as a girl in a harem. She can recall dancing naked, wearing only jewels.

Gunther used to shoot doves. Do you remember eating those? Just the breasts, ripped loose, and the rest simply thrown away. Sometimes my scribbling here feels like picking at the dregs of those same tiny bird bones, and — ha! — loads of gristle to get around.

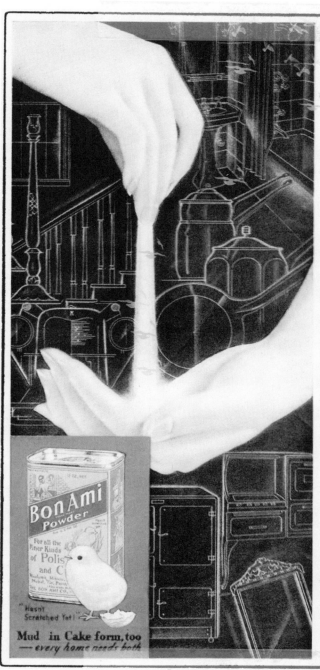

Try this
finger tip
test . . . . .

Scuttle-butted hopes
in the bird tracks.
Wednesday world
chews Tuesday world's
knuckles, then scolds
a bitter Thursday
for biting its nails.

What did we do to
tick off the Februaries?
What now? First the
journey calls. Then it
comes for you.

Bon Ami
Powder

For all the
Finer Kinds
of Polish
and C

"Hasn't
Scratched Yet!"

Mud in Cake form, too
— every home needs both

137

Here's your Grandnan Ruth
hamming it up! She was at
business college for a year.
I think this was then. Before
Sherry, of course, or even your
father. Before the last war
started. She just recently
sent me this picture. I guess
she still thinks she's got
herself some nice legs. She's
78 this year. Tap-dancing her
way to the moon.

139

I wish I could recall who took this picture. I was never very good on my side of the saw. Chester did most of the work.

I've made for myself this little busyness of the book, and I wonder did I wait too long? My fingers get sticky from the glue on these faces. I can never seem to get them smooth enough in their slots. I doubt any here had the least idea these expressions would be what outlasted them. I can't tell a crease from a scar on someone's cheek. There seemed a lot more to everyone's story when I first began.

Someone here is very, very dead. It happened overnight. Her heart, we guess. It ticked down to its last tock. Yesterday she raised a hand as Jasmine wheeled me past her room, and now I'm wracking my brains to recall if I even said hello.

Hello, Lizzy. I've been saying that all morning. I was saying it when they rolled her down the hall with a white sheet pulled up over her face. Hello, Lizzy. They tried to shut my door before they took her off, but I told them, "Please don't." What do they think they're hiding?

By noon a ferocious blizzard has filled my windowsill with snow.

When I asked Jasmine if she thinks Polina's baby will be more of a noise than an actual child, she didn't laugh or smile but said quite matter-of-factly, "Whatever comes out will offer great shrieks to the world."

I can't help but agree. I think I'd like to hold an infant one more time in my arms before I go.

When he started working on it, I gave
your Uncle Buddy maybe a hundred
reasons his minotaur game was
preposterous, but he'd only laugh.
Now everyone says he's going make
a million dollars and go live in
Long Beach with Randall. They want a
sailboat. Well, who doesn't?

This was something I found to give
Buddy and probably forgot to. Jasmine
will tape it in for me. The white
bull that mated with a queen of Crete
to create this creature, the quake
that obliterated Knossos — Buddy
seemed certain his company wouldn't
want any of that incorporated into
the game.

Today we're sitting around waiting to
hear something about a stint. They
might try to put such a thing in my
heart. Honestly, what will they think
of next?

143

I started this book in 1994, the year you started Butte High, and I planned to give it to you when you graduated, but a lot happened in those four short years. As you well know! Much water over the old dam.

One of these boys was Chester's brother, but I couldn't tell you which. He went to high school for nearly ten years! He'd quit to haul hay and then he'd go back. Chester used to say it was really so he could play football. Their team made state champion more than once. Chester's brother never missed a game. I believe even a year ago I'd have remembered his name.

Mildred says she will mail this to you when I'm done. She is a kind person, although we disagree on matters of god. She is probably praying right this minute for my soul. Ruth called and said you're no longer in France but in Canada. Canada! And just WHAT, pray tell, might be in Canada? Or maybe WHO?

I trust so little anymore but I have to believe this will reach you. I suspect I've gotten a few names and many of the dates wrong. Forgive me. Bean flowers and moon flowers blur in my memory; so do honeymoon bells and mice playing behind walls.

Everything is rushing together as I try to reach the last page. Mildred brought me a mailing box. Poor thing, she has her own people to pray about. I hope I have a right address for you in Canada.

144

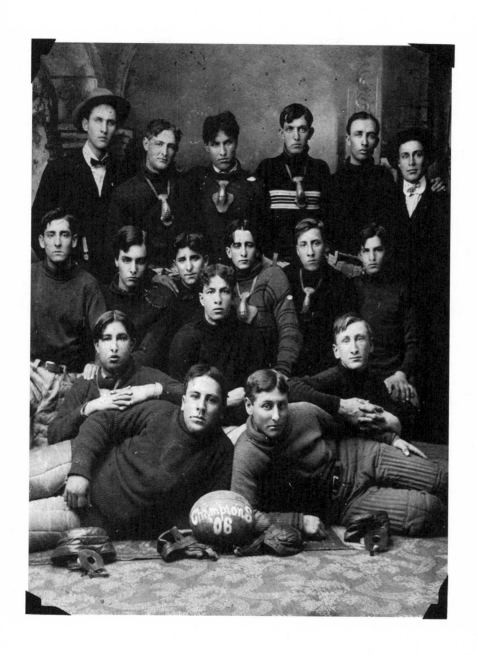

145

Whatever happened
with this picture is how
I feel sometimes as the
last page nears. And
aren't Chester and I
rather ghost-like
here at Glacier
Park?

About ten years after his first wife died, Mr. Clark married a lovely Butte gal — from French Town — Anna Eugenia La Chapelle. As a child, she'd been his ward. They had two daughters, and this is the one (Andree) who died of meningitis at 16. The other one must be nearly my age and is supposedly still carrying on, something of a recluse, I read in the paper, out in California.

A person's wrong leg is amputated
by mistake. You hear such horrible
tales about hospitals. After I lost
my breasts your mother joked that
something might have been accidentally
left inside me — a rubber glove or a
sponge. She thought that sort of talk
was witty, but I confess she got me
wondering. To this day it crosses my
mind . . . a sharp something's been
left deep within . . . one of those
tiny blades . . . .

Another thing I recall about the Clark
house was the Sisters of Mercy taking
it over. Did I ever tell you how they
turned the ballroom into a chapel?
Stories about the sisters would curl
your toenails. With a terrible mauve
color they painted over Mr. Clark's
beautiful murals on the master bedroom
ceiling. I suspect the coporeal love
in the murals made them mourn all they
were missing. Some of the sisters
were quite young. They said they were
married to God and wore gold wedding
bands to prove it! I see that shade of
mauve anywhere, and I catch my breath
as I did when I first saw it, stepping
into that wondrous room and thinking
of the color of a new scar, a fresh
determined scar.

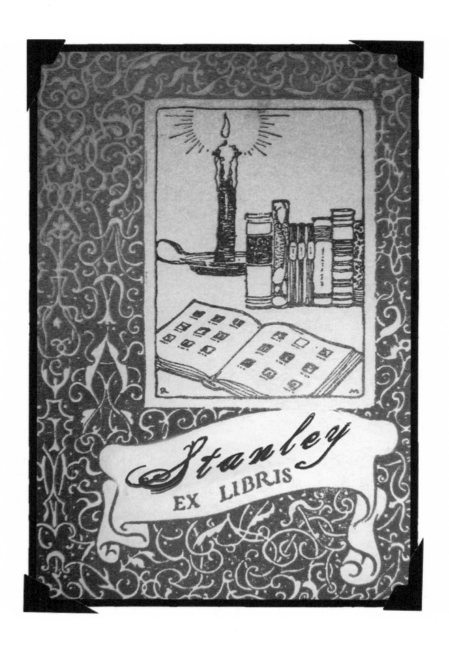

Stanley

EX LIBRIS

150

My family, the Stanleys, had books around, some they'd brought from England, but such was not the case for Chester's family, the Pettybones. They were all caring Christian people, Catholics. Thankfully the Homer Club brought books again into my life. A mere hour in a book sometimes seemed a day's reward. Chester often asked me to read him a half page I'd liked. After he died I remember coming upon a paragraph and thinking, Oh, now here's one Chess might like. For years I'd read a sentence aloud, imagining his face listening, that wan smile, a laugh waiting to spill over. He laughed so easily, and when he did, well whoever heard him just had to laugh too.

CYGNUS CHANGÉ EN CIGNE, & LES SOEURS DE
PHAETON EN PEUPLIERS.
*Cygnus transformed to a Swan, and Phaeton's
Sisters into Poplars.*

Cygnus in einen Schwaan, und die Schwestern des
Phaëton in Pappeln verändert.
Cygnus in een Swaan, en de Susters van Phaëton
in Populier-boomen verandert.

152

This book started out to be more
about our family but has become
almost as much about our family's
collection of monsters. Didn't
you color some of these with your
Grandnan and me when you were small?
These old pages were in my sack with
the photos. Maybe you can throw them
away. I couldn't.

That swan has himself some very
nice legs, and I so like these women
becoming poplars. Their grief for
their murdered brother Phaeton was
too much for them as simple women.
Evidently trees handle grief with
more grace, and clearly with greater
candor.

In the Homer Club we read about
these matters. People kept quitting
the human world. They mostly seemed
to like it when they do. I think
about that from time to time. We
were a family who admired the beast
hurtling out from within. Wouldn't
you agree?

STOP Thumb Sucking

Thumb sucking can be immediately corrected with the

Baby Alice Thumb Guard

Safe, sanitary, comfortable. Made of Monel Metal wire. Inexpensive. Approved by leading baby specialists. Sold by surgical dealers, department stores and baby shops—everywhere.

Guard Mfg. Co. 5 West 74th St. Cincinnati, Ohio

I believe the second Mrs. Clark used one of these on one of the daughters.

And oh yes, here's something you may appreciate knowing. It's about your Uncle Duke. His bones could never go in the consecated gound at Saint Al's.

Back when I believed, I used to pray for him.

He raised rabbits. Do you ever dream of rabbits? I did as a child and still do. My father raised them in Dakota. For roasting. They are such quiet creatures and only squeal that one time at the very end. A bite of one, just roasted, slides right off the spit and into your mouth.

Mrs. Axelrod also has a gift for
Polina. It's obviously a rattle.
We hear it in the box as she heads
to the elevator. She waddles AND
rattles!

Jasmine and I agree that we have
not cared much for Mrs. A., but now
we can't NOT like her. We'd thought
she was a hard woman, but she has
opened her heart.

Jasmine made Polina a basket
that's also a bassinet. A lovely
thing, woven of a lavender jute. I
insisted Jasmine remove the glass
beads she'd sewn in the trim.

As she clipped them free, we were
laughing, agreeing Mrs. Axelrod's
gift was the only one appropriate for
a tiny whistle.

    The faces here hardly seem like the
ones I knew. These two people were my
parents. But they're so young, barely
your age, newly married, not even having
sailed away yet from merry old England.
My father probably hasn't had the first
thought of a sea voyage, or of Virginia,
or the ranch that didn't last long in
North Dakota.

    I didn't know these young people, and
I smile to think of course they'd never
know me either, their own daughter, if
they saw me today on the street.

Your mother never liked my coffee. She once said, "Grandy, if you're going to make a French roast, you ought to use a French Press." I never knew anyone so sure how the world worked. Years ago she stuck this photo on my fridge: Our Lady of the Rockies. I took it right back down, but here I come to find it in this box of photos.

Our Lady Of, we called her in the H. Club, where I once let slip a phrase about her being "hard cold steel." What dark looks I received. When you were a toddler, you used to call her "Arlaney" and pretty soon all your little cousins believed that was her actual name. Seeing her up there on the top of the mountain, I used to think how she stood between me and my people on the other side of the Cont. Divide, all the family I was coming to realize I'd never see again, and me not giving any of them a proper farewell. My punishment is not being able to call back my own mother's face, or my father's.

Possibly some cousins of Chester's
A Nettie thing...

A funny thump - pause - thump in my heart
and Jasmine wants us to hurry and finish
this page so we can go downstairs and see
Polina today.

Apparently the baby hasn't come yet. When
I asked if there'd be any steps involved,
Jasmine said, "No, it's elevator all the
way."

I just like to recognize what'll be
required so I can muster my strength,
a concept young people can't quite
understand.

I've crocheted a yellow cap for the baby.
Though knit caps ARE nicer, my eyes
aren't good enough to knit anymore.

But my old knuckles can still
wrangle a hook, even
the tiny one for baby things.

Jasmine's typing especially fast so
I suspect there'll be many mistakes.
I AM hurrying.
I'm hunting down a nice
little box and a bow.

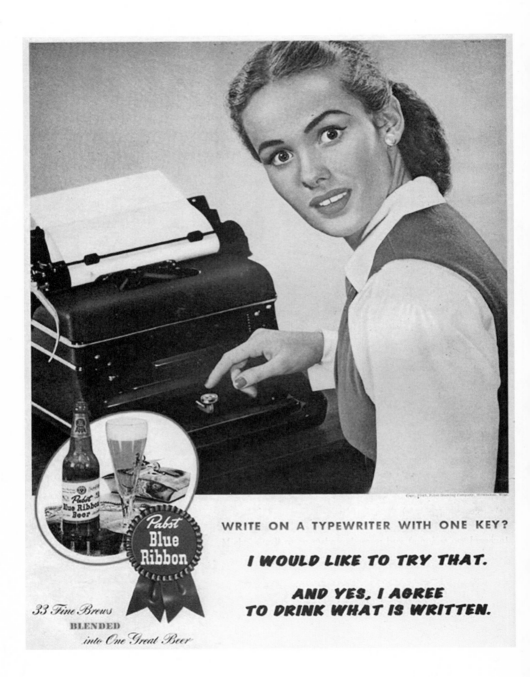

160

About the Author

Nance Van Winckel is the author of four collections of linked short stories and a recipient of a Christopher Isherwood Fiction Fellowship. Her stories have been published in *AGNI, The Massachusetts Review, The Sun, The Kenyon Review,* and other journals. She's also published six collections of poems, including *After A Spell,* winner of the 1999 Washington State Governor's Award for Poetry, and the recently released *Pacific Walkers* (University of Washington Press, 2013). She's received two NEA Poetry Fellowships and awards from the Poetry Society of America, Poetry, and Prairie Schooner. Nance's text-based photo-collage work has appeared in *Handsome Journal, The Cincinnati Review, Em, Poetry Northwest, Diode, Ilk,* and *Western Humanities Review.* She is Professor Emerita in Eastern Washington University's graduate creative writing program, as well as a faculty member of Vermont College of Fine Art's low-residency MFA program. She lives near Spokane, Washington with her husband, the artist Rik Nelson.